MULGA BILL'S BICYCLE

Poem by

A. B. PATERSON

Illustrated by

KILMENY & DEBORAH NILAND

Parents' Magazine Press • *New York*

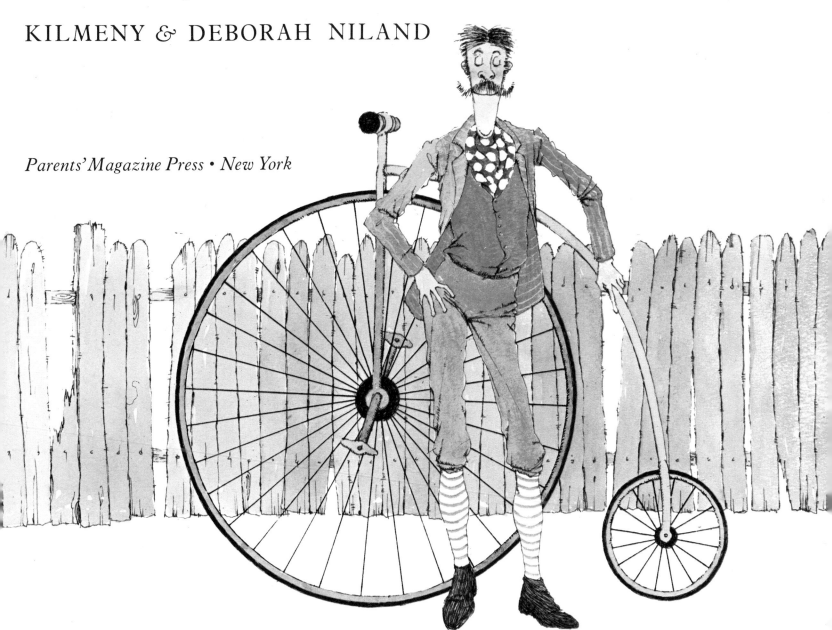

Library of Congress Cataloging in Publication Data

Paterson, Andrew Barton, 1864-1941.
   Mulga Bill's bicycle; poem.
   SUMMARY: Mulga Bill turns away his good old horse
and gets a bicycle, much to his regret.
   [1. Bicycles and bicycling—Fiction. 2. Australia—
Fiction. 3. Stories in rhyme]. I. Niland Kilmeny,
illus. II. Niland, Deborah, illus. III. Title.
PZ8.3.P2725Mu5   [E]   74-12286
ISBN 0-8193-0777-7   ISBN 0-8193-0778-5 (lib. bdg.)

'Twas Mulga Bill, from Eaglehawk,
who caught the cycling craze—

He turned away the good old horse that served him many days.

He dressed himself in cycling clothes, resplendent to be seen,
Then hurried off to town and bought a shining new machine.

And as he wheeled it through the door,
      with air of lordly pride,
The grinning shop assistant said,
      "Excuse me, can you ride?"

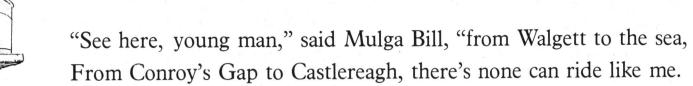

"See here, young man," said Mulga Bill, "from Walgett to the sea,
From Conroy's Gap to Castlereagh, there's none can ride like me.

"'He's good all round at everything,' they say of me in toasts,
Although *I'm* not the one to talk—I hate a man who boasts.
But riding is my special gift, my chiefest, sole delight;
Just ask a wild duck can it swim, a wild cat can it fight.
There's nothing clothed in hair or hide, or built of flesh or steel,
There's nothing walks or jumps or runs, on axle, hoof, or wheel,
But what I'll sit, while hide will hold and girths and straps are tight.
I'll ride this here two-wheeled concern right straight away at sight."

'Twas Mulga Bill, from Eaglehawk, who sought his own abode,
That perched above the Dead Man's Creek, beside the mountain road.

He turned the cycle down the hill and mounted for the fray,
But ere he'd gone a dozen yards, it bolted clean away.

It left the track, and through the trees, just like a silver streak,
It whistled down the awful slope towards the Dead Man's Creek.

It shaved a stump by half an inch,

it dodged a big white-box:

The very wallaroos in fright went scrambling up the rocks.

The wombats hiding in their caves dug deeper underground,

But Mulga Bill, as white as chalk, sat tight to every bound.

It struck a stone and gave a spring
that cleared a fallen tree,

It raced beside a precipice as close as close could be,
And then, as Mulga Bill let out one last despairing shriek,

It made a leap of twenty feet into the Dead Man's Creek.

'Twas Mulga Bill, from Eaglehawk, who slowly crept ashore.
He said, "I've had some narrer shaves and lively rides before—
I've rode a wild bull round a yard to win a five-pound bet,
But this was sure the derndest ride that I've encountered yet.
I'll give that two-wheeled outlaw best; it's shaken all my nerve
To feel it whistle through the air and plunge and buck and swerve.

"It's safe at rest in Dead Man's Creek—we'll leave it lying still;
A horse's back is good enough henceforth for Mulga Bill."